For my nieces
Emma and Charlotte

First published 1994 by Walker Books Ltd
87 Vauxhall Walk, London SE11 5HJ

This edition published 2009

2 4 6 8 10 9 7 5 3 1

© 1994 Zita Newcome

The right of Zita Newcome to be identified as author/illustrator of this work
has been asserted by her in accordance with the Copyright, Designs and Patents Act 1988

Printed in China

British Library Cataloguing in Publication Data:
a catalogue record for this book is available from the British Library.

ISBN 978-0-7445-3517-4

www.walker.co.uk

Just Like Me!

Zita Newcome

WALKER BOOKS
AND SUBSIDIARIES

LONDON · BOSTON · SYDNEY · AUCKLAND

Seal plays with a ball,
just like me.

Mouse curls up small,
just like me.

Frog jumps up in the air,
just like me.

Tiger prowls everywhere,
just like me.

Penguin goes flip flip flap,
just like me.

Crocodile goes snip snip snap,
just like me.

Horse can gallop and prance,
just like me…

But none of them can dance
just like me!